Baseball Flyhawk

BASEBALL
FLYHAWK

by Matt Christopher

Illustrated by Foster Caddell

Little, Brown and Company
BOSTON   TORONTO

Published simultaneously in Canada
by Little, Brown & Company (Canada) Limited

PRINTED IN THE UNITED STATES OF AMERICA

To

TONY AND MID

1216258

Baseball Flyhawk

1

THE score was tied, 4-4, as the Royals came to bat in the top of the fourth inning.

"Buddy! Chico! Dale!" Coach Pete Day named off the first three batters. "Come on! Let's get a man on! Let's break this tie!"

Buddy Temple picked up a yellow bat and walked to the plate. Chico Romez selected his favorite brown one, put on a helmet, and knelt in the "on deck" circle. Sweat shone on his face. It was a hot day for the opening game.

But it wasn't the heat that bothered Chico. He could take the heat. He was

3

born in Puerto Rico, had lived there six years before moving to New York City. And it was always hot in Puerto Rico.

No, it was the way he played baseball that bothered him.

The best way to make people like you was to do something that would please them. Chico thought that by playing good baseball he would make a lot of friends. But so far in this game, he had done nothing to please anybody. Not even himself.

Buddy took a called strike. Then he blasted a single through the pitcher's box.

The Royals fans cheered and whistled.

"Okay, Chico," said Coach Day, and rubbed the front of his shirt.

The bunt signal was on.

Chico stood at the plate, the bat held over his shoulder. He was short and not too husky. But he was fast. If he laid one down he might make it to first.

The Braves pitcher toed the rubber and hurled in the ball. It was low, slightly inside. Chico put out his bat.

Tick! The ball fouled to the backstop screen.

The next pitch was high. Again Chico tried to bunt.

Foul! Strike two!

"Hit away, Chico!" said the coach.

Chico rubbed his toes in the dirt and held his hands close to the knob of the bat. He had failed to bunt. Now he just had to hit.

The tall Braves pitcher stepped on the rubber, looked at Buddy on first, then delivered.

The pitch was high. Chico let it go by.

"Ball!"

The next was in there. Chico swung. A drive over short! Chico dropped his bat,

sped to first. Buddy crossed second base and headed for third.

Chico touched first, and continued on toward second. The ball was bouncing out to left field. He was sure he could make it. His legs were a blur as he ran.

"Chico!" yelled the first-base coach. "Get back!"

But Chico thought that he had gone too far to turn back now.

The left fielder picked up the ball, pegged it to second. The throw was straight as a string. The second baseman caught it, put it down quickly in front of the bag, and Chico slid into it.

"Out!" snapped the base umpire.

Chico looked puzzledly at the umpire and at the second baseman. Then he rose and trotted to the dugout, slapping the dust off his pants.

"One base was enough on that hit,

7

Chico," said Coach Day. "Shouldn't have tried to stretch it."

"I'm sorry," murmured Chico.

"Sorry!" echoed somebody on the bench. "A lot of good that'll do."

That was String Becker. Everybody called him String because he was tall and thin. He was the Royals first baseman, the most popular player on the team.

Chico blushed and sat down at the end of the dugout. It was indeed foolish of him. Making a stupid out like that just made matters worse.

2

CHICO looked at Buddy on third. Well, if he had bunted he might have got out, anyway. And Buddy would now be on second instead of third.

Catcher Dale Hunt stepped to the plate, and popped to third for the second out.

Frankie Darsi, the Royals' southpaw pitcher and one of the best in the Grasshopper League, came up and drew a walk. Now the head of the batting order was up again, shortstop Ray Ward. Ray was small. He couldn't hit very well. But first time up he had drawn a walk. The second time up he had struck out. This time everybody hoped he would walk again.

The Braves pitcher threw in two perfect pitches, putting little Ray on the spot. He hit the next one directly at the pitcher, who threw easily to first for the third out.

"Tough luck, Ray," said Coach Day.

The sad look on Ray's face, though, showed that the words gave him very little comfort.

"Hurry in! Hurry out!" snapped the plate umpire.

Frankie walked the first man to face him. String Becker yelled to the infielders to make some noise, and they all began chattering at once.

A strikeout and two pop-ups ended the Braves' chance to score.

Center fielder Joe Ellis led off the top half of the fifth. He grounded out to short. Dutch Pierce smacked one out to deep center for a triple, and the fans came to life.

This was the Royals' chance to break the tie. String Becker was up.

String threw left and batted left. So far he had blasted a double. His second time up he had hit a high one to right field that was caught. It was no wonder now that the fielders shifted to the right and stepped farther back.

String took the first pitch. A ball.

He swung at the next one. *Crack!* The ball sailed high and deep . . . deep . . . deep! The right fielder went back . . . back. . . .

Over the fence went the ball for a home run!

"Hooray! Thataway, String! Nice blast!"

The fans stomped their feet on the stands. String crossed home plate, a smile on his lips from ear to ear. Every member of the team was waiting for him to shake his hand.

11

The Royals now led, 6 to 4.

Right fielder Billy Hubble walked. Buddy and Chico grounded out to end the inning.

"Let's hold them!" Coach Day yelled to his boys.

Frankie worked hard on the mound. He looked tired. The sweat rolled from his face. He kept wiping it with the sleeve of his baseball shirt.

One . . . two . . . three outs. The Braves hit each time, but into someone's hands.

The sixth and last inning. Dale Hunt singled. Frankie lined one to short. The ball was scarcely six feet off the ground. The shortstop caught it, pegged it to first, and Dale was out.

Double play!

Coach Day had Kenny Morton pinch-hit for Ray. Kenny singled through short. Then Joe Ellis struck out.

"All right, boys! This is it!" said Coach Day. "Plug up all the holes!"

"Let's hear the chatter!" cried String.

The Braves lead-off man struck at the first pitch. *Crack!* A high foul ball directly over Dale's head.

He waited for it to come down. Caught it! One out.

Then Frankie got a little careless. Perhaps it was because he was tired. He walked the next man. The next pounded out a single, a Texas leaguer over second. String called time and walked to the mound. He said something to Frankie, then returned to his position at first.

The Braves fans were yelling excitedly, trying hard to offer encouragement to their players.

Chico, in left field, felt his heart pounding hard. With two men on, the Braves could tie the score and go on to win.

"Strike him out, Frankie!" he yelled. "Strike him out!"

A left-hand hitter stepped to the plate. The fielders moved slightly to the right. Frankie pitched.

The batter swung. Bat met ball, and Chico saw the little white pill soar high into the air. It sailed toward left field about halfway between Chico and the infield!

Chico ran in hard. "I got it!" he yelled. "I got it!"

For a moment he wasn't sure he would get it. He ran harder. Then he put out his glove, and the ball dropped into it.

"Great catch, Chico!" yelled Dutch Pierce from third.

"Thataboy, Chico!" He heard String all the way from first.

Chico's heart tingled.

He ran back to his position. *It was a good thing I caught that ball,* he thought.

He felt so good about it he didn't think about the batter who came to the plate. The Braves' number one slugger. A right-hand hitter.

Frankie breezed in a pitch and the tall Braves hitter smacked it. The ball left the bat as if it were shot from a gun. Chico could tell instantly that it was going over his head.

He turned around and started running as fast as he could. It wasn't fast enough. The ball dropped and bounced on. By the time he picked it up and pegged it in he was too late.

It was a home run. It won the game for the Braves, 7 to 6.

Chico trotted in from the outfield. He heard someone shout his name, saying things that sank deeply inside him and hurt.

"Where were you playing for that man? Behind shortstop?" It was String Becker. His face was red with rage.

"I was playing my right position," murmured Chico.

"Right position, my eye!" shouted String. "You weren't playing deep at all. If you were playing where you should've been, you would've caught that ball easy."

Chico stared at the others around him. One by one they turned and looked away.

They all felt as String did. They blamed him for losing the game.

3

CHICO," said Coach Day, "help me put this equipment away, will you?"

"Okay, Coach."

They put the catcher's equipment, the bats and the balls into the large canvas bag.

"Don't take to heart what String and the other boys say," advised the coach. "They don't really mean it."

Chico frowned. "Then why do they say —" He didn't finish.

"They just forget themselves for a minute," said the coach. "They get kind of excited. I'll talk to them about it."

17

"No, Coach. Please. Do not say anything to them."

"Why not?"

Chico shrugged. The sun shone brightly in his eyes, making him squint. "I do not want them to think I spoke to you about it. They — they wouldn't like that."

Coach Day smiled. "Okay. If you say so. Want a ride home?"

"No, thanks," said Chico. "I live only two blocks away."

The coach got into his station wagon and drove off. Chico walked, his glove swinging from his wrist.

He got to thinking about the way String yelled at him, and the way the other boys looked at him. *I'm a Puerto Rican, that's why*, he thought. *Every little mistake I make, they make it sound much worse.*

He was abreast of Jim's Ice Cream Bar when a voice from inside yelled to him.

"Hey, Chico! Come in. Have a soda."

Chico looked through the screen door and saw six or seven members of the Royals sitting at the bar, enjoying sodas. It was Buddy Temple who had called to him.

Chico glanced quickly over the faces. He saw String Becker, and that was enough.

"No, thanks!" he said, and started walking faster.

A moment later Buddy was out on the sidewalk, yelling to him. "Chico! Hey, Chico!"

But Chico walked on, not looking back once.

He reached home, went to the back porch, and sat down. His heart pounded as if he'd been running. His forehead was covered with sweat. He wiped it with his arm.

Then he looked at the glove in his hand and sucked in his breath.

This wasn't his glove!

He rose to his feet, trembling. Whose glove was it? And what had happened to his?

A lump rose in Chico's throat. What an opening day this was for him! He had been blamed for the loss of the Royals' first game. Now he had come home with somebody else's glove.

The door behind him opened on squeaking hinges. He turned around. His mother smiled at him.

"Chico! When did you get home?"

"A little while ago," said Chico. He turned and sat down again, his lower lip quivering.

She came and sat beside him. "Chico, is something wrong, my son?"

He told her about the game, and the glove. Her dark-brown eyes looked at him sadly. She put an arm around his shoulder and pressed him to her.

"Do not worry so," his mother said. "You will find who owns the glove, and you will find yours. It was only a mistake." She stood up. "Come inside, Chico. You must be hungry."

Chico washed, changed into other clothes, then sat at the table in the dining room. On the wall behind him was a large white cloth on which were embroidered the Spanish words DIOS BENDIGA NUESTRO HOGAR. And underneath it, in English, GOD BLESS OUR HOME.

Chico's father came in from the living room. His hair was black and wavy. His eyes, behind thick-rimmed glasses, were brown and smiling.

21

"Your face looks sad, Chico," Mr. Romez said. "You lost the ball game?"

"Yes," said Chico. "A home run over my head in the last inning beat us."

"That's too bad," said his father. "Well — better luck next time."

While he ate the meat and beans and the tossed salad, Chico worried about his glove. Had somebody else picked it up? Was it the person who owned the glove he had picked up?

Chico couldn't swallow his food for a minute. Why was he always doing something wrong?

Then he thought about his teammates. Especially String. String, Chico was sure, didn't like him at all.

But he remembered something, and with pride he thought: *At least I can do one thing well. And I have two trophies to prove it!*

There was a knock on the door. Mrs. Romez went to answer it.

"Chico," she called, "someone to see you!"

Chico stared. The trembling returned.

4

THE boy at the door was Buddy Temple.

"Hi, Chico. How about coming over after a while? We can play catch, and I'll show you my electric train set."

Chico's face lit up. He turned around to his mother and father. "May I?"

His mother smiled. She looked at her husband. He smiled, too, and nodded.

"Good!" said Buddy. "I'll see you later, then." He started to leave.

"Buddy," said Chico, "wait!"

Chico went to the kitchen and returned with the glove he had picked up by mistake.

"I brought this glove home," said Chico. "But it's not mine. Do you know whose it is, Buddy?"

"Well, I know it's not mine," replied Buddy. He took it, looked closely at it, then unbuttoned the straps and looked at its underside. "No name on it. No, I don't know whose it is, Chico. Keep it until the next game. Somebody should claim it then."

"Okay," said Chico. "But somebody has mine, too. Didn't you see one of the boys with a different glove, Buddy? Didn't anybody say anything?"

Buddy shook his head. "No, I didn't, Chico. But don't worry. You'll get yours back. And you'll find the owner of that one, too. See you later, Chico!"

Chico watched Buddy hop off the porch and head for home. A smile touched his lips. All at once he wasn't lonely any more. He liked Buddy Temple. And he knew Buddy liked him.

He went to Buddy's house later. They played pitch-and-catch. Then Buddy took Chico into the basement and showed him his electric train set. It was on a large table — the size of a ping-pong table — and stood about two feet off the floor. The trains were all kinds — passenger, freight, cattle cars. Buddy turned on a switch on one of the two transformers and the passenger train began to move along the track. He turned on a switch on the second transformer and the freight train began to move. The trains crossed bridges, went through tunnels, passed by tiny buildings.

"Whoo-o! Whoo-o!" their whistles shrilled.

Chico watched with fascination as the

freight train stopped and a cargo of "cattle" moved off a loading platform onto a car.

"Maybe someday my father will buy me a set like this," said Chico hopefully.

Buddy smiled. "My dad started this for me a long time ago," he said. "Every Christmas he gets me something new. It's lots of fun. Especially in the winter."

"I must go home," said Chico. "May I come again? I never saw a train set like this before."

"Of course, you may come again, Chico." Buddy's eyes were warm, friendly. "Any time."

The next day Chico thought about his glove, and the one that didn't belong to him. *I hope it is not String's. And I hope he does not have mine.*

Then he realized that it could not be

String's glove, because String's was a first base mitt.

Chico went to the swimming pool at the park in the afternoon. His mother went with him. There were two diving boards, one low, the other high. Chico climbed up the high one. He stood on the tip of the board, the sun warm against his body.

He stretched his hands straight out in front of him, looked down at the water, and saw his reflection in it. A smile cracked his lips, then he gave himself a spring and dived off the board.

He struck the water like a whisper, went to the bottom, and came up, blowing air out of his lungs.

"Nice going, kid!" the lifeguard said. Chico smiled back.

He stayed there a long time, diving and swimming. He forgot about String, and his glove. Being in the water took his mind off all his worries.

Came the day he dreaded. The moment he was afraid to face. The day of the second game.

He saw most of the Royals players at the first-base side of the field, warming up. The Colts were behind third. Chico looked around anxiously. Everybody had a glove and was playing catch.

"Let's hit!" Coach Day yelled. "Fielders, get out there! Buddy, lay one down and hit two! Kenny, throw 'em in!"

The fielders scrambled to the field. Kenny Morton walked to the mound and began pitching them in.

Chico stood there a moment, holding the glove that did not belong to him. Then he started trotting out to the outfield.

"Hey, Chico!" a voice suddenly yelled behind him. "Come here!"

Chico stopped in his tracks, whirled. Dutch Pierce was walking toward him. He had just come onto the field. He was looking with dark, piercing eyes at the glove on Chico's hand.

"That looks like my glove," Dutch snapped. He whipped it off Chico's hand. "It is!" His eyes blazed as he looked at Chico. "Where did you get it? How long did you have it?"

Chico stepped back. Dutch was four inches taller than he.

"I — I picked it up by mistake after our first game," he stammered.

"By mistake? What a story that is!" Dutch's lips tightened. "Crook!" he said, and ran out to the field.

For a moment Chico stood there, trembling.

Where is my glove? he thought, and began to worry more than ever.

5

"CHICO."

Chico turned, and squinted against the sun at Coach Day.

"There's a glove inside the equipment bag," said the coach. "It's probably yours."

Chico ran to the bag, opened it, and pulled out a glove. It was his!

"Thanks, Coach," he murmured. "I — I was afraid I would not find it."

Coach Day grinned. "You had left it lying on the ground, and had picked up Dutch's. If I'd known it was yours, I would have taken it to you. Okay, get your hits now, then shag a few."

After the Royals had their hitting practice, the Colts took the field. A little while later the game started.

The sky was clear blue and the sun a bright, blazing ball of orange. A perfect day for baseball.

The Royals had first raps. On the mound for the Colts was Teddy Nash, a tall, freckle-faced southpaw. His warmup pitches breezed in like white bullets.

Lead-off man Ray Ward strode to the plate. Teddy Nash made short work of him. Joe and Dutch didn't get to first base, either. It looked as if Teddy was going to have a good day.

Out in the field Chico realized that he and the other fielders might have some trouble. They had to face the bright sun.

Don Drake, a right-hander, pitched for the Royals. He walked the first man and then the second. The third man hit into a double play. Then a single scored a run. Catcher Dale Hunt caught a foul pop fly and the first inning was over.

String Becker was first man up for the Royals. He swung two bats from one shoulder to the other as he walked toward the plate. He tossed one back and stepped into the box. He tapped the plate with the big end of his bat, then waited for Teddy Nash to pitch.

Teddy blazed two over the plate. String swung at both and missed. Then Teddy wasted a couple, making the count two and two.

"Come on, String! Make it be in there!" said the coach.

The next pitch was in there. String belted it, a hot grounder down to first. The first baseman reached for it. His mitt touched the ball, but it went through for a hit. String dashed to first.

"Okay, men, there's our starter," said the coach. "Let's keep it up."

Billy Hubble tried. So did Buddy and Chico. But Teddy's ball was working for him. None of the three hit, and String died on first.

The game continued swiftly along. Both pitchers were hot. Teddy's ball had no curve to speak of. But he had a side-arm delivery that made it seem as if the ball were coming from near first base. Most of the Royals players were shy of the ball, thinking it would hit them. But Teddy's control was fine, and the pitches were strikes most of the time.

Don's delivery was overhand. He had learned to throw two curves. One was a "screwball," a pitch that curved in toward a right-hand batter. The other curved away. This one was better, for it had a drop to it, too.

In the fourth inning things began to pop. Teddy got a three-two count on Dutch, then threw an inside pitch that dusted Dutch off. A free ticket to first for Dutch.

String came up. So far only he had got a hit off Teddy Nash. Teddy blazed in two pitches, both balls. Then String took a called strike. The next pitch was in there, too, and String powdered it. The ball sizzled just inside the first-base line for a clean single. Dutch went around to third; String held up at first.

"Okay, boys," said Coach Day. "Two ducks on, and none away. Let's bring them in."

Billy Hubble tagged the first pitch. It was a pop fly in the infield, an automatic out.

The boys in the dugout groaned.

Buddy waited till a strike was called on him, then socked a chest-high pitch down to short. A perfect throw to first put him out.

"Come on, somebody!" yelled String disgustedly. "Can't anybody hit that ball?"

It was Chico's turn to bat. He started for the plate.

"Chico! Wait!"

Chico turned. His jaw sagged. He looked pleadingly at the coach. *Don't let somebody pinch-hit for me*, he thought. *I am sure I can hit that ball now.*

Chico started back toward the dugout.

"No, never mind," said the coach, waving Chico back to the plate. "Get up there, Chico. Show 'em you can do it."

A sudden happy gleam entered Chico's eyes. He turned, went to the plate, and dug his toes into the dirt.

"Strike one!"

Chico thought that the pitch was a little inside.

38

Then — there it was — coming in belt-high. Crossing the plate almost down the middle. Chico swung. *Crack!* A long, high blast going over the left fielder's head!

Chico dropped his bat and ran. One run came in! Another! Chico crossed first, second, and went to third. The third-base coach waved him on to home. Chico kept going, his black hair flying wildly on his head. Somewhere on the base paths he had lost his helmet and cap.

"Stay up, Chico! Stay up!" cried the men crowding around home plate, waiting to shake his hand.

A home run!

"What a smack, Chico!" String said. "Nice —"

Suddenly there was silence. One of the Colts infielders was drawing the attention of the men around the plate.

"What's he saying?" Coach Day asked wonderingly.

"He's out!" cried the umpire at first.

"Who's out?" said Coach Day. No one else spoke. Even the bleachers were silent as the fans watched, wondering what had happened.

"That kid who just hit that home run," said the umpire, running in and pointing at Chico Romez. "The first baseman saw it, and I saw it. He never touched first base!"

Chico stared. His heart sank to his shoes.

"What a crazy, stupid thing!" yelled Dutch. "A home run — and he didn't touch first base!"

6

THE score was still one to nothing in the Colts' favor.

Chico's heart was crushed. He wished that Coach Day would remove him from the game. He was so ashamed of the foolish mistake he had made he didn't care if the coach benched him for the next two or three games.

But the coach left him in.

"Watch it the next time, Chico," advised Coach Day. "Touch every base."

"Yes, sir," murmured Chico. But it was like locking the barn after the horse had run away.

The Colts got a man on. Their long ball

hitter was up and Chico stepped back deeper into left. *Crack!* The white pill shot toward left center field as if from a cannon. Chico and center fielder Joe Ellis raced after it.

Somebody from the infield yelled, "Let Chico take it! Let Chico take it!"

Chico reached out his glove, caught the ball, and just missed colliding with Joe. He pegged the ball in.

"Beautiful catch, Chico, boy!" The fans applauded him.

Then a ground ball went for a single, and the Colts scored a run. Two to nothing, Colts' favor.

In the top of the fifth Dale singled. That gave the Royals a starter. They went ahead and scored. String made the last out of the inning.

Don's hooks baffled the Colts hitters.

Not a man reached first. The close game kept the fans on edge.

This was the Royals' last chance.

Kenny Morton pinch-hit for Billy Hubble, and whacked a double. Coach Day put in another pinch-hitter, Louie Carlo. Louie took a strike, then popped up to the pitcher. One away.

Chico strode to the plate.

"Come on, Chico! Another blast! Another homer! This time touch the bases!"

The pitch. "Ball!" said the umpire.

Another pitch. Chico powdered it — a ground ball through short. Kenny touched third, went in to home. Chico dashed for first, the fans' cheers ringing in his ears.

Chico made sure he touched first. He headed for second, his helmet flying off his head.

"Chico!" yelled the first-base coach.

"Play it safe! Watch that throw-in!"

The left fielder pegged the ball in to second. A perfect throw!

Chico, two-thirds of the way to second, slid to a stop. *What have I done?* he thought. The second baseman ran Chico back, then tossed the ball to the first baseman. Chico was caught in a hot box.

Back and forth the first and second basemen passed the ball to trap Chico. Then — suddenly — the first baseman's peg went wild! The ball hit the ground and bounced to the right of the bag. Chico raced to the keystone sack. Safe!

"Wow!" murmured Chico. He bent forward and put his hands upon his knees tiredly. *That* was sure close!

Dale popped out. Two outs. Then Don socked one over second. It was just out of reach of the second baseman, and Chico scored.

44

Ray Ward struck out. But Chico's run put the Royals ahead, 3 to 2.

"Hold them!" yelled the Royals fans. "Hold them!"

"Three men to get, Don, boy!" yelled String. "Just three!"

Don's hook fanned the first batter. The next hitter clouted one over short, a clean hit. The batter slid in to second safely for a double.

String called time. He went to the mound and talked with Don. Then he returned to first. Time in was called.

Don stepped on the rubber, delivered. A hot one-bouncer right back at him! Don caught it, tossed it to first. Two away.

One more to get!

A right-hander stepped to the plate. Don pitched. *Crack!* A long drive to left field. Chico started back, then turned and watched the white pill come down from the sky.

Suddenly it was lost in the blinding sun! For an instant Chico had a glimpse of it again. He put out his hand. *Whoosh!* The ball struck the glove's little finger, hit the ground, and bounced past Chico.

Chico ran after it, picked it up, and pegged it in. The throw was too late. The hitter was running home from third. He crossed the plate before the ball reached Dale.

The game was over. The Colts were the winners, 4 to 3.

"How did you miss it?" stormed String, his eyes fire-red. "You should have caught it easily!"

"It was the sun," murmured Chico. "It shine in my eyes."

7

THERE was something special about the day the Royals played the Lions. Small, fluffy clouds speckled the sky. The sun blazed like a golden coin. But those were not the things that made the day different.

Nearly every home on the streets had the American flag displayed in front of it. Some were suspended on staffs. Others hung from the ceilings of porches. They stirred in the breeze, little waves rippling through them.

Chico remembered seeing flags displayed once before. His family was living

48

in New York City then, on a very crowded street. All of their neighbors were Puerto Ricans, too. Many of them had moved from their land, far away on the island of Puerto Rico, to New York to live. Just as Chico's family had done.

Chico couldn't remember, though, why those flags were displayed that day. He had heard of Flag Day. Was it Flag Day?

"Is today Flag Day, Buddy?" he asked curiously.

He and Buddy were in uniform. They were hurrying to the baseball park.

Buddy smiled. "No. It's Independence Day, the Fourth of July. This is a big holiday, Chico. Everybody in the United States celebrates it."

"They all hang out the flag?" murmured Chico.

"Yes. Well, everybody who *has* a flag, that is," smiled Buddy.

Maybe it was the Fourth of July then, too, thought Chico.

A brass band was at the park. It was in the bleachers behind first base. Chico realized that something special was happening here today, too.

Both teams warmed up. Chico caught a glaring look from String. Matter of fact, nobody gave him a glad-to-see-you look. They remembered that he had lost the game for them last Thursday. That he had lost the ball in the sun was no excuse.

A few minutes before the game started both teams walked out to the infield. The Lions stood along the third-base line, the Royals along the first-base line. In front of them, standing near the mound, were the coaches of both teams. They all faced center field.

The band began to play "The Star-

Spangled Banner." The coaches and the players took off their caps and held them against their chests. On the tall flag pole near the center-field fence the American flag was going up.

Chico watched it while the music filled the park. There was something about the flag that warmed him all over. Something about it that was more than just a piece of cloth with red and white stripes and white stars.

When the song was over Chico felt a lump in his throat.

The game started. The Royals took the field first, with the lineup the same as last time. Only today, southpaw Frankie Darsi was on the mound.

Frankie blazed the ball in overhand and had no trouble getting the Lions out that first inning.

The Royals came up and scored two runs. In the third they scored three more to put them in the lead, 5 to 0.

"We'd better take this game," murmured String in the dugout, loud enough for everybody to hear. "We can't give it away now."

Chico felt that String intended those words especially for him.

In the top of the fourth the Lions threatened to put across some runs. Two hits in a row put men on first and third. Then Frankie walked a man and the bases were loaded.

The heavy hitters of the Lions were up. Frankie stepped on the rubber, delivered. *Crack!* The first pitch was smacked to deep left. Chico went after it. He knew what it would mean if he failed to catch this fly ball.

The ball curved toward the left-field

foul line, but it was still well in fair territory. Chico ran as hard as he could, put up both his hands, and caught the ball. He stopped quickly, pegged the ball in to third. Dutch caught it and tagged the runner bolting in from second.

The runner on third had scored, though, after tagging up.

"Nice throw, Chico!" Dutch yelled to him.

Five to one. Then a pop-up ended the Lions' threat.

Chico singled in the bottom of the fourth. He ran partway to second before the first-base coach's cries registered in his mind. "Get back here, Chico! Get back here!"

Chico got back to first. *Almost played it foolish again,* he thought.

Dale Hunt came to bat and blasted the first pitch. The ball streaked in a clothesline drive toward short. Chico took off. As he neared the keystone sack he heard loud shouting behind him. He looked out to left field, expecting to see one of the out-fielders fielding the ball.

But the ball wasn't out there!

Chico looked at the smiling face of the Lions second sacker and knew instantly that something funny had happened.

He turned, and saw the Lions first base-man standing on the bag, the ball in his hand.

Chico's eyes widened. "What happened?" he murmured.

"What happened?" The Lions second baseman laughed. "You're out, that's what happened! Our shortstop caught the line drive and doubled you off at first!"

Chico stared. He slapped his helmet angrily against his side and ran across the diamond to the dugout.

"Chico!" said Coach Day. "Why don't you watch it? That ball was in the air!"

"I am sorry," said Chico.

"Pulls a boner all the time!" exclaimed String disgustedly. "We'll probably lose this game yet."

But the Royals played airtight ball after that and went on to win, 5 to 2.

Chico saw his mother and father waiting for him, and walked home with them.

"Nice game," said Mr. Romez.

Chico shrugged. "It would be better," he said, "if I didn't pull boners!"

His mother and father laughed.

At the supper table Chico thought about the American flag. He asked his parents if the stripes on the flag meant anything.

"Of course," said his father. "The thirteen red and white stripes represent the thirteen original colonies of this country.

The stars represent the states in the Union. The flag is carried in battles and wars. It is a great symbol. We owe it much respect. It represents our unity and our freedom."

Mrs. Romez smiled. "In Puerto Rico we had the United States flag, too," she said. "It flew side by side with Puerto Rico's flag. You were too small to remember, Chico."

Chico looked at his mother and father and his eyes glowed happily.

Suddenly he remembered something, and the smile vanished from his face.

"Papa, we do not have a flag. Why not?"

His father eyed him thoughtfully a moment, then shook his head.

"We will get one, Chico. I am glad you reminded me. We will get one soon."

8

LATER that evening Chico thought about calling Buddy Temple to go swimming with him at the park. Then he decided that he'd rather go alone.

He took his bathing trunks, changed at the bathhouse, then climbed up to the higher diving board.

There were other kids swimming. The lifeguard was there, too, sitting on his tall platform. He smiled and waved at Chico. Chico waved back.

"Look out!" one of the kids in the water shouted. "Chico's going to dive! Let's see you do a back-dive, Chico!"

Chico smiled. He turned, placed his

heels close to the edge of the diving board, and sprang. He stretched his hands outward, and arched his back so that he looked like a graceful bird flying through the air. Then he put his hands together, and struck the water straight and silently as an arrow piercing a target.

"Nice dive, Chico!" the kids yelled, as he came to the surface.

"Thank you," he said.

He obliged them with jackknife dives, both frontwards and backwards, and then a somersault. He felt happy, now. He was doing something he could do well.

Perhaps someday he could do as well playing baseball.

Buddy Temple came over the next day with his glove and a ball. He and Chico played catch.

"How would you like to go with me on my paper route tomorrow morning,

Chico?" Buddy asked. "Mom, Dad, and us kids are going on a vacation for a couple of days. If you want to, you can deliver my papers for two mornings. All you earn those two days you can keep. How about it?"

"Sure, Buddy," said Chico. "I will do it."

Chico answered before giving it any thought. After all, Buddy was his best friend. He would help Buddy no matter what it was.

But — deliver papers? That bothered him. Would just one day of going around with Buddy help Chico remember all the customers?

"How many customers do you have, Buddy?" asked Chico.

"Sixty-four," said Buddy.

"Sixty-four!" Chico's eyes went wide.

Buddy laughed. "Some guys have seventy or eighty! It's not too bad. They're

60

all within a few blocks of each other. You won't have any trouble, Chico. Then you'll do it?"

Chico smiled. "Of course!"

"Thanks, Chico! You have to be up early! We must pick up our papers at seven o'clock."

"I'll be up," promised Chico.

The next morning Buddy was at the front door at ten minutes of seven. Chico was up, waiting for him. They walked two blocks to the corner of Hanley and Lincoln Streets. Four boys were there already, newspaper bags slung over their shoulders. They spoke to Buddy, but looked strangely at Chico.

"This is Chico Romez," said Buddy. "He's going to deliver my papers for me the next two mornings. My folks and I are leaving about six o'clock tomorrow morning. We're going to be gone for two days."

61

Buddy introduced the boys to Chico, and Chico felt better.

A few minutes later a station wagon drove up. A man got out, greeted the boys, and hauled out several piles of newspapers. The papers had a peculiar smell. Buddy said it was the ink.

Buddy explained to the man why Chico was with him, then piled the newspapers into his bag. Chico watched carefully.

Then the man took several tickets out of his coat pocket and gave one to each boy. Except Chico.

"For the Jay Jam Circus tonight," he said. He looked at Chico. "Sorry, boy. These are only for our regular carriers. We don't have any extras."

Chico shrugged. "That's all right," he said.

Chico and Buddy crossed the street. Buddy took the ticket out of his pocket.

"Here, Chico," he said. "You take it."

"No," said Chico. "It's yours. Why do you want to give it to me?"

Buddy looked at him a moment, then returned the ticket to his pocket.

He got back to his business of delivering papers. He showed Chico how he folded them and tossed them onto the porches.

Chico learned by doing. He folded the papers, too, and tossed them onto the porches of Buddy's customers the way Buddy did. It was fun.

It took almost an hour to deliver all the papers. Buddy took Chico home with him and gave him a list of names and addresses.

"There you are, Chico," said Buddy. "You can't miss. And here's the bag. Good luck!"

Chico smiled. "Thank you. With this

63

list I should not have trouble, Buddy."

Chico took the list and the newspaper bag home with him, and put them in his room.

That afternoon the Royals played the Marlins, and won 12 to 1. Errors and foolish plays took the heart out of the Marlins. The Royals' record now was two wins, two losses.

That evening Chico met Buddy, String, Frankie and Dale coming up the street.

"Hi, Chico!" said Frankie. "We're going to the circus. Can you come along?"

"I have no ticket," said Chico, sadly.

"No ticket, no circus!" laughed String. Chico glowered at him.

"Can you get some money from your dad, Chico?" asked Buddy. "You can pay him back out of what you'll make from selling those papers."

Chico smiled. "Maybe! Will you wait for me? I shall ask him."

"Go ahead," said Buddy. "We'll wait."

Chico ran into the house. His mother and father were both home. Breathlessly he asked them if he could go to the circus with Buddy, String, Frankie, and Dale.

His parents smiled. "You don't want to go with us?"

Chico's brows raised. His eyes widened. "You are going, too?"

His mother went to the cabinet in the dining room and brought out three tickets. "We were ready to leave in a little while," she said. "Would you rather go with us, or your friends?"

Chico stared. What a choice to make!

"I will go with you and Papa," he said, and started to turn away. "I will tell the boys."

"Wait, Chico," said his father. "Mama, give him his ticket. Let him go with his friends. I think he will enjoy it better."

Chico's eyes brightened. He took the ticket. "You sure it is all right, Papa? Mama?"

"We are sure," nodded his mother.

"Thank you!" he shouted, and ran out to join his friends.

The big tent of the Jay Jam Circus was packed with fun. Elephants danced, tigers and lions leaped through hoops, acrobats performed on flying trapezes, a man and a girl pedaled bicycles on a tight wire high above the ground. Chico had seen something like this on television, but this was the first time he had ever seen it live.

That night he went to bed thinking about those amazing performances. It was a long time before he fell asleep.

When he woke up the first thing on his

mind was the circus. He chatted about it with his mother as he ate breakfast. His father had already left for work.

Suddenly he remembered something. Something he had to do!

"Mama! Mama! What time is it?" he asked, jumping out of the chair.

"It's eight o'clock," she said.

"Eight o'clock?" Chico's heart leaped to his throat. "Mama! I am supposed to deliver Buddy's papers today. I should have been at the street corner at seven!"

"Oh, my poor boy!" his mother cried. "And look what is happening outside!"

Chico ran to the window, and choked back tears.

Raindrops, as big as nickels, were pouring from the sky.

9

CHICO put on his raincoat and rubbers. He folded the newspaper bag, put it under the raincoat, and ran out into the rain. Suddenly he remembered the list of names and addresses, and ran back into the house for it.

What a terrible thing to forget his promise to Buddy!

Horrible thoughts rolled around in his mind. Certainly the man who brought the papers would not be waiting for him. It was Chico's responsibility to be there at seven o'clock. One hour ago! The papers were probably soaked from the rain.

Chico's heart was never so sick.

He ran all the way to the street corner where the newspapers were supposed to be. There was no one there, of course. Not even a pile of newspapers.

Chico's eyes widened painfully as he looked around him. Hadn't the man left the papers?

Then he saw them. They were against the trunk of a tree where the rain could not hit them so heavily. Some old newspapers were draped over them, with a rock on top to keep the newspapers from blowing off.

Chico breathed easier. At least the man had thought about him a little.

Chico took out the newspaper bag, unfolded it, and piled the papers into it. When the papers were all inside, he took off his raincoat, picked up the bag and put the strap over his shoulder. Then he put the raincoat back on and started out on his route. The papers were heavy. The strap of the bag began to hurt his shoulders.

The raincoat helped to keep the papers from getting wet, but the paper containing the list of names became wet and soggy. Chico's thumb smudged some of the names, and he had difficulty reading them.

Little by little, though, the pain left his shoulder as the weight of the papers grew lighter. Once the rain slacked for a few minutes, and Chico thought it would stop. Then it poured again as heavily as before. It was still pouring when Chico finished delivering the papers.

At last! Not only was his shoulder light, his heart was, too.

But he still had tomorrow morning's delivery to make. He hoped it wouldn't rain then.

"You are home!" his mother exclaimed

as she opened the front door for him. "My poor boy! Were the papers all wet?"

Chico grinned through the rainwater that glistened on his face. "Not too bad, Mama. I had them covered very well."

It rained the rest of the morning. Chico wondered what to do to spend his time. He turned on the television, but nothing was on that interested him. He wished he had some books from the library. The magazines in the house were for Mama and Papa. The words were big. He didn't understand them. And he didn't care for the pictures.

Then he thought of something, and his heart hammered with excitement. He would draw the American flag!

His mother got him a large sheet of white paper. Then, in a book, he found a small picture of the flag and copied it with pencil. He drew the flag so that it covered the whole sheet. He colored it with crayons. When he was finished he held it up with a proud, shining light in his eyes.

He showed it to his mother.

"Very nice!" she said. "Be sure to let your father see it when he comes home."

It stopped raining just after dinner. Chico took the drawing outside. He hoped some kids he knew would come by so that he could show it to them. He heard laughter down on the next block, and recognized String Becker, Ray Ward, and Dale Hunt. They were playing, but what game it was Chico couldn't tell from here.

He walked down the street to them. He saw now what they were playing. They had made "airplanes" from sheets of paper, and were throwing them up into the air. The airplanes flew around in circles. They zoomed, dived, and then glided to a landing on the street or on the sidewalk.

"Hello, Chico," said String. "What've you got there?"

Chico smiled. String would be surprised at this. He wouldn't think that Chico, a boy who didn't know too much on the baseball field, would spend any time drawing a picture of the American flag. Chico held up the drawing.

"Well, look at that!" said String. "A picture of the flag. That's good, Chico! You do it?"

Chico nodded proudly.

String took it. "You didn't make the stars too good," he said. "Stars have five points. Some of these have only three or four."

Chico's smile faded slightly.

"And some of the red stripes are almost twice as wide as the white ones."

Chico's heart sank. He reached for the drawing.

"Wait a minute," said String. "This isn't so good. Let's make an airplane out of it. It's big, and it'll fly like an eagle."

"No!" said Chico. He reached for the drawing again.

String looked at him. "Don't you want to have a plane like we have?"

"Yes," said Chico. "But not out of the flag I draw."

String laughed.

Ray and Dale came up beside them. "It won't hurt, Chico," said Ray. "Let String make you a plane out of it. It's only paper, anyway."

A ball rose in Chico's throat. Paper? It was the American flag! His, and theirs! Should it make a difference if it was drawn on paper?

No words could come to his lips as he watched String fold the large sheet through the middle, then fold in the corners. A few moments later the flag was an airplane, with red and white stripes and white stars against a patch of blue.

The boys chuckled. "Looks like a fighter plane!" exclaimed Ray.

"Let's see how it works!" said String.

He hurled it as hard as he could. It leaped high into the air, curved, then shot down in a fast glide over the street.

"Man! Look at that bird fly!" cried String.

All four boys ran after it.

The airplane landed beautifully far down the street. No sooner had it settled on its side than a car came toward it.

"Watch it!" yelled Chico. "Watch it!"

The driver swung his steering wheel, but not soon enough. The front left wheel of the car ran over the airplane. The car slowed down, then picked up speed and continued on.

Chico rushed out to the street and stared down at what had been his flag.

It was crushed.

10

CHICO picked up the airplane. Wet imprints of the car's tire smeared its colors.

"It can still fly, I bet," String said. "Watch!"

He took it from Chico, straightened the wings a little, and threw it into the air. It flew gracefully around in a circle, then bumped the side of a house and dropped to the ground.

"See that?" said String. "That car didn't hurt it!"

Chico didn't answer. It wasn't an airplane. It was the American flag. *Every-*

body showed respect to the flag, Papa had said. But these boys didn't!

"You can keep it!" he told String, his happiness shattered. "I'm going home."

Chico went home and drew another picture of the flag. This time he was more careful. He made the stars with five points, and made the red and white stripes almost exactly the same width. When it was finished it looked better than the first one he had drawn.

A smile crossed his lips. Maybe it was a good thing he had shown his first drawing to the boys.

But he had another plan for this one. He found a couple of tacks, took the picture to his room, and fastened it on the wall above the head of his bed.

It was beautiful the next morning. The sun was out, birds were singing. Chico

arrived at the street corner ahead of time, picked up the newspapers, and went on his route.

He referred often to the list of names and addresses to make sure he delivered the papers to the right customers. He had written over the smudged names so that it was easy to read now. Today the job was fun.

Later that afternoon Buddy came over with a ball and glove. He wanted to know how Chico made out yesterday morning when it had rained so hard.

"I forgot about it," Chico said. "I woke up late. When I reached the corner it was eight o'clock. But the man put the papers under a tree and covered them up. I am sorry I was late, Buddy. But I delivered the papers okay."

Buddy smiled. "I'm sorry it rained, Chico. Of all the times!"

"Did you have a nice vacation, Buddy?"

"Wonderful," said Buddy. "My uncle has a boat. We had picnics, and rode around most of the time."

They played catch for a while, then Buddy went home.

The Royals tackled the Bombers on Tuesday. The game started with the Bombers' living up to their name. They knocked in three runs in the first inning, and two more in the second. They were pounding Don Drake's pitches all over the lot.

Frankie Darsi replaced Don. His southpaw delivery stunned the Bombers for a while. They either grounded out or struck out. The Royals came through with two runs in the third, one in the fourth. They clinched the game in the last inning when String smashed out a home run with two men on.

On Friday the Royals tangled with the Braves as the second round began. There were three rounds altogether.

Don Drake started on the mound. The Royals picked up two runs in the second inning. They held the Braves to two hits until the third inning, when Dutch Pierce fumbled a grounder that started things for the Braves. They socked out a double, scoring a run. A walk and then a wild peg to first by shortstop Ray Ward filled the bases.

The cleanup man stepped to the plate and smashed a long, powerful drive out to left field. It looked like a grand slammer!

Chico turned and put his back to the ball as he raced out toward the fence. Then he looked over his shoulder, turned, and made a sparkling, one-handed catch.

The runners tagged up. The man on

third raced for home. Dutch caught Chico's throw-in and held the ball. It was too late to get the man scoring the run. The other runners had advanced. So now there were men on second and third.

The fans cheered Chico's catch. "Thataway, Chico! Nice catch, boy!"

A one-hopper to Don, which he threw easily to first, and then a strikeout, ended the bad inning.

Score: Braves — 2; Royals — 2.

"Beautiful catch out there, Chico," Coach Day said as Chico trotted in. "You robbed him of a homer."

Chico smiled.

Buddy Temple led off and flied out to center. Then Chico came up. He took a strike, then smacked a grounder that just missed the pitcher's legs. A single!

Dale Hunt hit a sizzling grounder to third. The Braves third sacker bobbled the ball. By the time he had it in his hand it was too late to throw anywhere.

Chico stood on second, breathing hard. His right shoe felt loose. He saw that the laces had come untied.

He didn't want to call time out, though. He would wait until he got to the dugout, then tie the laces.

Don blasted the first pitch. A high fly to center field. The center fielder made the catch. Chico tagged up and made a beeline for third. He had to beat that throwin!

Then, halfway to the bag, his right shoe felt ready to fall off.

11

CHICO kept running hard.

Suddenly the third baseman reached out to the left side of the bag to catch the throw.

"Hit the dirt!" yelled the coach.

Chico slid. He went to the right side of the bag, hooked it with his left foot. Safe!

The fans roared.

Chico called time. He laced the shoe tightly and tied a knot.

Boy! If that shoe had come off, would not the fans have laughed then!

Lead-off man Ray Ward smacked the first pitch right over the first baseman's head for a clean single. Chico scored. Dale advanced to third.

Joe Ellis walked, filling the bases.

Time out was called, and the Braves manager came out of the dugout. He walked to the mound and motioned in another pitcher.

The new man was a southpaw. He was short, stocky, and had a lot of speed. After a few warmup pitches, the game resumed. There were two outs.

Dutch Pierce stepped to the plate. With String Becker on deck, the Braves' new hurler was facing the Royals' strongest hitters. Dutch took a ball, then smashed a chest-high pitch over second base. Dale scored, followed by Ray Ward. Joe Ellis held up at third.

That clout, and those scoring runs, did not make the Braves southpaw look very happy. His infielders came in and talked with him. When they returned to their positions he walked up on the mound and faced the Royals' hardest hitter, String Becker.

He looked around the bases. There were men on first and third. You could tell he wished anybody else was at bat but String.

The little southpaw stepped on the rubber, made his stretch, and delivered.

String swung, and missed. "Strike one!"

The southpaw breezed in another. String started to swing, but didn't.

"Strike two!" said the umpire.

String stared at him, but didn't say anything.

Another pitch. String swung hard. *Swish!*

"You're out!" shouted the umpire.

String stood at the plate a moment, staring at the little southpaw. Then he tossed his bat aside, got his first-base mitt from the dugout, and trotted out to his position. Not a word left his lips.

"That's all right, String," said the coach. "You'll be up again."

Chico knew that was quite a blow for String. Imagine a little southpaw striking out String Becker!

The score now was Royals — 5; Braves — 2.

Coach Day had Kenny Morton take Buddy's place at second and Louie Carlo take Joe Ellis's place in center field.

The Braves came up in the top of the fourth, anxious to do something about the score. A single and then a sacrifice bunt put a man in scoring position, but the Royals' defense was working fine today. Not another man reached first.

The Royals hit hard at their turn at bat, but always into somebody's hands.

Nothing serious happened until the sixth, when the Braves made a last desperate attempt to raise their score.

They managed to put across a run, making the score 5-3. Now, with two outs and two men on, they had their best chance of tying it up — or even going ahead of the Royals.

Their cleanup hitter was up. Already he had knocked out two doubles.

Anxiously, Don Drake looked toward the dugout at Coach Day.

"Pitch to him, Don," said the coach.

Chico backed up in left field. Louie Carlo stepped back, deeper in center. This batter was a long-ball hitter. If he met the ball squarely, it would go.

Chico waited.

12

CRACK!

The sound of the bat connecting with the ball was like a shot. The white pill streaked out to deep left, curving toward the foul line.

"It's going over the fence!" someone in the bleachers yelled. "It's a homer!"

Chico raced back. Near the fence he turned, looked over his shoulder. The ball was coming down a few feet inside fair territory. It was over his head.

He leaped high. *Smack!* The ball struck the pocket of his glove and stayed there.

Chico trotted in with the ball. His heart hammered with triumph. Ahead of him

his teammates were jumping with joy. Fans were cheering.

"Beautiful catch, Chico, boy! Nice leap!"

"You saved the game for us, Chico!" Coach Day's eyes and face were bright as Chico approached. "Best catch I've seen in months!"

"Thank you, Coach," Chico said. And then he stood there while every member of the team shook his hand. String was last in line. He gripped Chico's hand lightly, then let go.

Chico was sure that String shook his hand only because the others did.

That night Buddy came to visit Chico. He and Chico went over the list of batting averages. String was leading with a whopping .397. Buddy's average was .388, Chico's, .297.

"String is a much better hitter than us,"

said Chico. "I wish I can hit as good as he."

"Who doesn't?" said Buddy.

Chico thought about it awhile. "I will try harder," he said finally. "Maybe if I hit better, String will not make so much fun of me. I know he does not like me."

"Oh, sure he does," said Buddy. "That's just his way, Chico. He's always yelling at guys."

Chico shrugged. He remembered how lightly String had gripped his hand that afternoon. "I guess I'm strange," he said.

Nevertheless, he made up his mind to use a different bat. Maybe he couldn't beat String's average, but it would not hurt to try.

On Monday the Royals played the Colts. When Chico batted, he gripped the long, yellow wood near the knob and swung at the pitches with all his might. The bat was an inch longer than the one

94

he had used in previous games. It was the same size String and some of the bigger boys were using.

But the bat didn't help Chico. He struck out.

The next time he was up he hit a dribbling grounder to the pitcher. He made a "shoestring" catch of a fly ball, though, that kept the Colts from scoring two runs. The Royals squeezed through with a win, 8 to 7.

Chico went without a hit.

In the game against the Lions, Chico used the same long bat. He was sure he'd clout the ball today. Just one pitch — the right one — was all it took to blast it over the fence.

But Chico didn't clout the ball. He hardly touched it. He went down swinging twice.

"C'mon, Chico!" yelled String. "Quit

aiming for that fence! You'll never hit it then!"

Chico blushed.

On top of his poor showing at the plate, he also missed a high fly in the field that accounted for one of the Lions' runs. It was a bad day for Chico. Coach Day took him out in the fourth inning, and put in Louie Carlo.

"You're trying too hard at the plate, Chico," said the coach. "You're too tense."

Chico, though, knew what his trouble was better than anyone.

13

THE LIONS blasted Frankie off the mound in the fifth inning. Don Drake held them to three hits, but the Lions were roaring today. They took home the win, 9 to 3.

Perhaps, thought Chico, he had better not use the long, yellow bat any more. He would use the one he always batted with. Even though he never socked a homer with it, he had been able to get hits. And that's what counted most.

On Monday they played the Marlins. After the game, the boys were going to a picnic at Orchard Falls Park.

The Marlins had a right-hander on the mound, Dick Mills, who could throw sharp curves and knucklers. Chico wasn't worried. He was confident he could hit any curve or knuckler the pitcher threw up to him. He was going to use his old bat again.

"These guys are a cinch," String Becker said. The Royals were sitting in the dug-out, watching the Marlins take their in-field practice. "We trounced them twelve to one the first game. We ought to do it again."

"We'll make it a shutout this time," smiled Dutch Pierce.

The infield practice got over, and the game started. Dick Mills mowed Ray and Joe down with curves, but he couldn't fool Dutch. Dutch blistered an inside pitch past the third baseman for a single. String acted anxious to send one over the fence, but four balls gave him a free ticket to first.

This was a chance for the Royals to score. But with two strikes on him, Billy Hubble swung at a knuckler that must have looked as big as a balloon to him. He struck out, and the sides changed.

The Marlins lead-off man punched out a single over short and then stole second. An error on shortstop Ray Ward put another man on. The man on second stayed there.

"C'mon! Some life!" yelled String at first base. "Let's get 'em!"

Frankie worked hard on the third man, a left-hand hitter. A one-bouncer came back at him. Frankie caught it, spun, whipped the ball to second. Ray stepped on the bag, then pegged to first.

A double play!

The cleanup hitter was a tall, husky

right-hander. Chico moved back a dozen steps in left field. He remembered the first game with the Marlins. This guy had driven one to deep left. If it hadn't gone foul it would have been a homer.

Crack! The ball whizzed out to left field like a torpedo. Chico stepped back a little, and caught it easily. He knew that if he had not played deep for that hitter, he would not have caught that ball.

"Nice catch, Chico," Coach Day said as Chico came running in. "Pick up a bat. You're up after Buddy."

Buddy singled.

Chico walked to the plate. He was using his regular bat now. He was sure he could hit whatever pitch Mills threw to him.

"Strike!" He had let that one go by.

Another pitch. A hook. Chico swung. Missed.

"Strike two!"

Chico stepped out of the box, and the umpire called time. Chico adjusted his belt, pulled his helmet down tighter, and stepped back into the box.

Mills threw two more pitches, both balls. Now the count was two and two.

The next pitch came in. A hook. Chico swung. Whiff!

"Strike three!" said the umpire.

Chico turned glumly, tossed his bat and helmet aside, and walked back to the dugout. He shook his head. He couldn't understand why he had missed those pitches. He just couldn't.

Dale Hunt flied out. Then Frankie started a rally with a hot single through short. The Royals scored twice before the Marlins got them out.

Chico was up again in the third. String and Billy were on base. This was a chance for him to get some RBI's.

"Strike one!"

"Strike two!"

Chico couldn't believe it. Those hooks looked so easy to hit.

Then came the knuckler. The ball turned so slowly you could see the seams. Chico swung.

"You're out!" shouted the umpire.

Angrily, Chico tossed his bat aside as if it were the bat's fault that he didn't hit. He trembled as he returned to the dugout. He was ashamed to face anyone.

"That's all right, Chico," Coach Day said comfortingly. "You're too anxious. You'll hit it."

In spite of Chico's failure to hit, the Royals picked up two more runs. Then the Marlins pushed across three runs at their turn at bat, making the score 4 to 3, Royals' favor.

The Royals scored twice again in the

fourth, bringing their score to 6. Chico ended the inning by popping up. At least this time he had a "feel" of the ball.

Chico ran out to the field, wondering what he was doing wrong. He tore up a handful of grass, and flung it angrily behind him. Three times at bat and not one hit!

The Marlins began to hit and drove in a run. Then a man laid down a neat bunt toward third. Neither Frankie nor Dutch could get to it in time.

As Frankie released the first pitch to the next batter, the runner on first stole second. Dale didn't make the play on him. The man on third might try to run home.

The score was now 6 to 4. There were two men on, and no outs.

Chico saw the next batter come to the plate, but he paid him little attention. He was thinking about his own hitting. It seemed impossible that he couldn't hit that big, fat ball Mills threw. You would think he had never hit before!

Frankie stretched, pitched. *Crack!*

Chico saw the ball shoot into the air toward left — *deep* left. His eyes widened, and just for an instant he glanced at the batter who was now scrambling for first base.

It was the Marlins' slugger! Their long-ball hitter!

Chico turned and raced back as fast as his legs could carry him. He looked over his shoulder, and saw the ball streak over his head! It hit the ground, bounced to the fence. Chico ran after it, picked it up, and pegged it in.

Dutch Pierce caught it, relayed it home. The runner was racing in. He slid, dust exploding in front of his feet. Dale put the ball on him.

"Safe!" yelled the plate umpire.

A home run!

Chico felt terrible. It was his fault. He had thought so much about his poor hitting, he had neglected to watch who was batting.

Kenny Morton took his place after that, but neither team scored again. The Marlins won, 7 to 6.

String Becker glared at Chico as they walked off the field.

"You lost the game for us, you know that?" he cried. "You knew that guy hits a long ball. Why didn't you back up when he came to bat?"

"I know. I'm sorry," said Chico.

"Sorry, yeah!" said String with disgust. "That helps a lot now!"

14

A LL right, boys!" said Coach Day. "Don't forget the picnic at Orchard Falls Park!"

Chico headed straight toward the gate. His head was down. String's strong words were still ringing in his ears.

"Chico!" yelled the coach. "You're coming to the picnic, aren't you?"

Chico turned and paused. Yes, he wanted to go. But if everyone blamed him for losing the game, why should he? How could he enjoy himself?

"Come on, Chico!" said Buddy. "We'll hike and swim and have a lot of fun."

"Sure!" said Coach Day, smiling. "Don't

worry about today. It's all over with. Get home, change your clothes, and I'll pick you up in fifteen or twenty minutes."

Chico thought about it a moment. "Okay" he said, "I'll be ready."

Orchard Falls Park was ten miles beyond the city limits. A huge playground area was on the right side as you drove in from the highway. Farther in was the large pool. Sitting atop a high platform, a sun helmet on his head, was the lifeguard. He was busy watching the swimmers.

Beyond the pool were the high, frosty-white falls. A heavy mist hovered near the bottom where the water dropped with a loud, steady roar.

Scattered in dozens of places under the trees were picnic tables and fireplaces. Three cars, including Coach Day's station wagon, hauled in the boys. They found two empty tables close to each other and put them end to end. Then the men began to prepare the dinner.

Most of the boys dashed to the bathhouse, where they changed into their bathing suits.

"I don't care about swimming now," said String to Buddy. "Let's go on a hike along the gorge."

"Okay!" said Buddy. "Want to come along, Chico?"

"Does he have to go every place you go?" String snorted.

Buddy smiled. "No. But he's never been here. Have you, Chico?"

Chico shot an icy look at String. String was always making fun of him. "That's all right, Buddy. You two go alone."

"Never mind. Come on," said String. "I'm only kidding."

Only kidding. He always says that, thought Chico. *But I know he means it.*

I hope something happens to him so that he can't play baseball any more. He is too wise.

"I just hope we don't come across any snakes," said String. "I hate them!"

"I don't like them, either!" laughed Buddy.

They told Coach Day where they were going, then started toward the woods. Near the foot of the falls they found the path that led up into the steep, tree-filled hillside.

They paused awhile and watched the water gush over the falls. The thunderous roar made it hard to hear anything else.

They went on, climbing higher and higher. String and Buddy walked side by side, with Chico trailing behind them. On both sides of the path were dead, smelly leaves, pine cones and broken twigs.

Chico felt excitement bubbling inside

110

him. There was adventure here, and danger. Danger, because the steep path was slippery from the rain that had poured the other day — and only inches to their left was the sharp drop of the gorge.

"How far are we going?" asked Chico.

String turned. His eyes mocked Chico. "What's the matter? Getting scared?"

"No. But maybe the dinner is ready. By the time we get back —"

"Don't worry," said String. "There's plenty of food for everybody."

Chico shrugged. He was sorry he had said anything.

They continued slowly up the path, looking at the water below them, and the seagulls flying around in slow, lazy circles.

Suddenly something on the ground caught Chico's eyes. It was at the edge of the path — a snake about three feet long!

"Look out!" he screamed. "Snake!"

Just as he yelled, it slithered across the path behind the two boys. Buddy spun, his eyes wide, staring. String spun around, too. His face turned white. He saw the snake and jumped back.

One foot slid onto some leaves at the edge of the path, and he lost his balance. He fell, and slid on his back down the steep bank. He tried to stop himself, but couldn't. He screamed again.

The next instant he was falling through space, his feet sprawled out in front of him. Far below he struck the water and disappeared.

15

"HE sank! He's out of sight!" cried Buddy. Panic was in his face and eyes.

Chico was unable to move. Horror glazed his eyes as he looked at Buddy. "Buddy," he said, "I wished something would happen to String so that he could not play baseball any more! But I did not mean it!"

"Don't be foolish," said Buddy. "That was an accident. Golly, Chico — what are we going to do? He'll probably drown!"

Quickly, Chico started stripping off his clothes. "I will dive in after him," he said.

"Dive in? Are you crazy? That's about thirty feet! You can hurt yourself bad!"

"I won't get hurt," Chico assured him.

Buddy stared down at the water. "Look!" he pointed. "There's String! He came up! But he looks . . . he looks unconscious, or something."

Chico removed all his clothing except his shorts. Carefully, he hurried down the bank a few feet, stood in diving position for a moment, then pushed himself forward. He dived gracefully, his feet together behind him, his hands stretched over his head and spread slightly apart. It seemed a long time that he was suspended there in the air, holding his breath. Then he struck the smooth, mirrorlike top of the water. He went down deep, and swam back up to the surface.

The water was cool, and he shivered. He gulped in fresh air, whipped his hair

115

away from his face and looked around for String.

About twenty feet away from him — in the direction of the falls — he saw String bobbing in the water.

"String!" Chico yelled. "String!"

String paid him no attention. Terror took hold of Chico. Maybe Buddy was right. String was probably unconscious!

Chico started swimming as swiftly as he could toward String. The falls were not too far away. If he didn't get to String soon . . .

The horrible thought of what would happen made Chico swim even faster. Suddenly, he didn't see String. String had gone down!

No! There he was again!

Chico swam harder than he had ever swum in his life. The gap between them closed swiftly. At long last he reached

String, put his left hand under String's chin, then turned and swam toward the shore.

The current was strong against them, but Chico swam with powerful strokes. He reached the shore, pulled up String beside him with panting breath, and held String's head in his arms.

String's eyes were closed. He was breathing hard.

"String!" Chico cried. "String! Can you talk?"

"Who — who is it?" murmured String.

The words were like music to Chico. His eyes brightened. "It's me! Chico!"

"Chico? Boy! That snake really scared me! Where — where is Buddy?"

"Up on the path. Maybe he went after Mr. Day."

String didn't say any more. Chico looked at his wet face. It was pale and

118

tired. Chico grew worried. Would String be all right?

After a long while he heard voices nearby. Presently Coach Day and the other men came hurrying along the narrow shore. They saw him and String and rushed forward.

"How is he, Chico?"

"He was talking to me," said Chico.

"Good! Here, let me have him." Coach Day put his arms around String's shoulders. "String! Are you all right?"

String turned his head. His eyes opened. "I guess I swallowed a lot of water, Coach. My stomach feels full."

Coach Day smiled. "We'd better get you to a doctor, String. From what Buddy told us, that was quite a long fall."

"Chico saved my life, Coach," said String. "He dived in after me. That took a lot of nerve, Coach. You know it?"

16

THE doctor could find nothing seriously wrong with String, except that he suffered slightly from shock. However, he advised that String be sent to a hospital.

String stayed in the hospital only a day. He was told, though, that he should rest for a week. During that time the Royals played two games. They squeezed a win over the Bombers, 8 to 7, and lost to the Braves, 5 to 2.

Chico got a hit in each game. He felt he was getting back in stride.

On August 3 the Royals played the Colts. With String back on first base, the

Royals were their old selves again. But no, thought Chico. Something was different from before.

The Colts pounded Frankie's pitches, but a Royals man was always there to catch the ball. Their defense was like a brick wall.

The fans gave String a rousing cheer when he stepped to the plate. There were two men on. It was a good chance to score.

String took two strikes, then went down swinging. Ground balls to short and first ended the Royals' threat. The Colts were playing well defensively, too.

The innings went on without a score. The game turned into a pitchers' duel. Several men from both teams got on bases, but tight playing kept them from scoring.

In the fifth the Colts made another strong threat. The first batter singled, and stole second. Then Frankie threw a hook that went wild. The runner raced to third.

"Let's settle down!" yelled Coach Day.

String and Dutch Pierce walked to the mound to talk with Frankie. They returned to their positions and started a steady flow of infield chatter.

Out in left field, Chico watched the batter closely. Here was a strong hitter, he remembered. He didn't hit the ball very high, but low and hard.

Crack! A smashing hit to left. It sailed over third baseman Dutch Pierce's head in a long clothesline drive.

Chico moved back. The ball was coming like a bullet. It was going over his head!

He leaped. *Plop!* He had it!

The runner on third tagged up and made a beeline for home. The way the game was going, that run could mean plenty. It could win the ball game.

Chico reared back and pegged the ball in as hard as he could. It went over Dutch's head, bounced once, and Dale caught it. He tagged the runner.

"You're out!" yelled the umpire.

The Royals fans screamed and banged on the bleachers with their feet.

"Beautiful peg, Chico!" Dutch called.

"Thataway, Chico!" String shouted from first. "Great arm!"

Chico glowed with pride.

The next man grounded out and the inning was over.

With one out, String came to the plate. This time he cut hard at the first pitch and struck it solidly. Even as the ball sailed far and high, everybody just knew where it was going.

It went over the fence! A home run!

The next two innings were scoreless. The game ended, 1 to 0.

The whole Royals team crowded around String and Frankie. They happily pounded their backs and shook their hands. String's smile stretched from ear to ear.

Then he saw Chico. He came forward and put an arm around Chico's shoulders.

"Boy, Chico!" he said. "You really threw that apple! It was perfect!"

"Thank you," smiled Chico. "You really hit that apple, too!"

"Thanks, Chico. Look, after you change clothes and eat, come over to my house, will you? I have something for you."

Chico nodded. "Okay!"

He knew now what was different from before. It was String.

At home Chico took off his uniform, put on clean clothes, washed, and ate. All the while he wondered why String wanted him to go to his house.

It was almost twilight when he left. He met Buddy on the way, and Buddy went with him. Chico didn't think String would mind.

"Hi, Chico. Hi, Buddy," said String, as he opened the door for them. "Come in."

The boys sat in the living room. String left the room for a minute. When he returned he had something in his hand. An American flag!

It wasn't large, but it was larger than the one Chico had drawn and hung up in his room.

"Here. This is for you," said String. "I got one for me, too."

Chico stared. "But why?" he said.

"Just because," said String. "Here. Take it. On holidays you can show it outside. That's what I'm going to do."

Chico took it, held the metal staff out straight so that the flag hung like a curtain.

He could see that it was made of good cloth. And the colors were bright as could be.

"My folks did not buy one yet," said Chico. "Now they won't have to."

String smiled happily.

Things were working out fine, thought Chico. Just fine.